The Steadfast Tin Soldier

· H A N S · C H R I S T I A N · A N D E R S E N ·

The Steadfast Tin Soldier

I L L U S T R A T E D   B Y

· F R E D · M A R C E L L I N O ·

R E T O L D   B Y   T O R   S E I D L E R

◆

· M I C H A E L   D I   C A P U A   B O O K S · H A R P E R T R O P H Y ·

For Jean

—F.M.

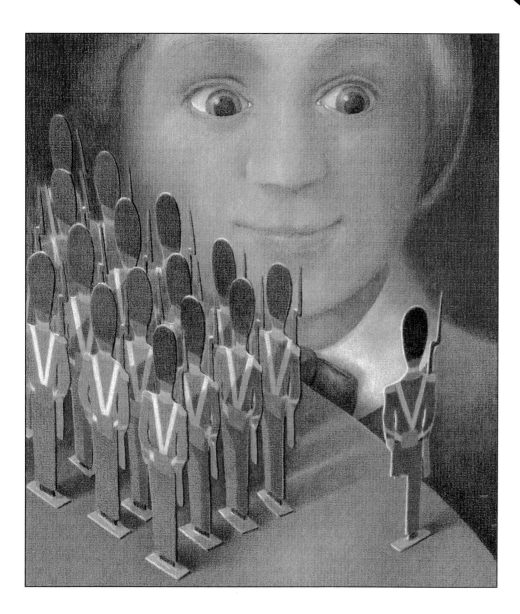

ONCE UPON A TIME there were twenty-five tin soldiers. They were all brothers, for they had all been made out of the same old tin spoon. The very first thing they ever heard was "Tin soldiers!" So cried the little boy who opened the box they came in. He clapped for joy and immediately started setting them up on the table.

They all stood at attention in splendid red-and-blue uniforms, rifles on shoulders, each exactly like the others—except for one. This soldier had only one leg. He was the last to be cast, and the tin had run out. But he stood as steadily on his single leg as the others did on two—and of them all, he was the one destined for greatness.

There were a good many toys on the table, the most impressive among them a handsome cardboard castle. You could see its elegant rooms through the windows, and in front of the castle was a glimmering lake—a piece of mirror, actually—surrounded by little trees. There were even wax swans floating on the lake, admiring their reflections.

It made a charming scene. Yet the most enchanting thing of all was the girl standing in the castle doorway. She was only made of paper, but her dress was fluffy gauze, and she wore a narrow blue sash held in place by a shiny spangle as big as her face. Her arms were outstretched, for she was a dancer, and one of her legs was lifted so high behind her that the tin soldier couldn't see it at all. It looked to him as if she, too, had only one leg.

"What a perfect wife she would make for me!" he thought. "But she might be too grand. She's used to a castle. It would be hard to ask her to move into a box with me and my twenty-four brothers. Still, I wish I could get to know her." There was a snuffbox on the table. From behind it, the tin soldier had an excellent view of the lovely dancer, who kept standing on one leg without ever losing her balance.

Later that evening, all the other tin soldiers were put back in their box, and the people who lived in the house went to bed. It was then that the toys began to play.

They threw parties, and fought battles, and danced. The tin soldiers rattled in their box, eager to join the festivities, but they couldn't get the lid off. The nutcracker turned somersaults, and a piece of chalk squeaked on a slate. They all made such a racket that the canary woke

up and started chattering away—in verse, no less! The only ones who stayed quite still were the tin soldier and the little dancer. She remained balanced on the tip of her toe with her arms stretched out. He was just as steadfast on his single leg, and his eyes never left her for a second.

All of a sudden, when the clock was striking midnight, the lid flew off the snuffbox—*bang!*—and out sprang a goblin. The snuffbox wasn't a snuffbox at all! It was a jack-in-the-box.

"Tin soldier!" cried the goblin. "Keep your eyes to yourself!"

But the tin soldier pretended not to hear.

"Just you wait till tomorrow!" the goblin said.

W

hen morning came, the children got up, and the tin soldier was set on the window sill.

Before long, a gust of wind—or was it the goblin?—blew open the window and the tin soldier tumbled out. It was a terrible fall, three stories to the street below. The poor soldier landed headfirst, his bayonet stuck between two paving stones, his leg in the air.

The little boy and the house-maid rushed down to the street to look for him. They came so close they nearly stepped on him. If the soldier had just called out "Here I am!" they would have spotted him, but he was in uniform and didn't think it proper to shout.

They had to give up the hunt when it started to rain. The drops fell thicker and thicker. Soon it was a downpour.

Once the rainstorm was over, a couple of street urchins came strolling by. "Hey, a tin soldier!" one of them said. "Let's see what kind of sailor he makes."

So they folded some newspaper into a boat, put the tin soldier on board, and sent him off down the gutter. The rain had swollen the gutter stream, and the boys ran alongside the fierce current, clapping their hands as the boat tossed and turned and twirled. The tin soldier was getting seasick, but he remained steadfast, eyes front, his rifle on his shoulder.

Suddenly the boat was swept under a long plank covering the gutter and everything went black. "Now what?" the soldier wondered. "This is as dark as inside our box with the lid on. And it's all that goblin's fault. If only the young lady were with me! Then I wouldn't care if it was twice as dark."

Just at that moment, out popped a huge water rat who lived under the plank. "You have to pay the toll," the rat declared. "Hand it over!"

But the tin soldier said nothing. He just held his rifle tighter. The boat rushed on and the rat raced after it, gnashing his teeth furiously. "Stop him!" the rat screeched to the twigs and straw. "He hasn't paid the toll!"

The current was picking up speed, and the tin soldier saw a patch of daylight up ahead.

But he also heard a roar that would have chilled the heart of the most courageous hero. The end of the plank was the end of the gutter.

There the water poured down into a great canal. Going over the edge would be like going over a tremendous waterfall.

It was too late to stop. The current hurled the boat over the brink. Yet even then, the tin soldier remained at attention. No one could ever accuse him of flinching, not for a single second.

In the canal the boat whirled around and around until it filled up with water. It was doomed. Once the poor tin soldier was up to his neck, the newspaper began to fall apart under his foot. As the water closed over his head, he thought of the lovely dancer he would never see again, and an old barracks song rang in his ears.

Brave soldier, never fear,
Even though your death is near.

The boat broke to pieces and down he went. No doubt he would have sunk into the mud at the bottom of the canal if a fish hadn't swum by just then and swallowed him up.

Inside the fish was the darkest place yet, even worse than under the plank. What's more, there was hardly a breath of air. But the tin soldier lay

there steadfast as ever, his rifle still on his shoulder.

All at once, the fish began to twist and turn in the most terrifying way. Finally, it grew perfectly still.

19

What seemed like a streak of lightning flashed, and then it was broad daylight. "The tin soldier!" someone cried. The fish had been caught, taken to market, sold, and brought to a kitchen, where the cook had sliced it open with a big, gleaming knife.

After clearing dinner, the housemaid picked the soldier up by the waist and took him into the living room. The whole family crowded around to see the remarkable fellow who had been on a voyage in the belly of a fish. The tin soldier wasn't the least bit proud of himself. Yet what an astonishing place the world was! For here he stood, back on the same table as before, surrounded by the same children and the same toys, including the castle with the lovely dancer in the doorway.

The dancer was still balanced on one leg, the other still held high: She, too, was steadfast. The tin soldier was so touched that he would have shed tin tears—if he hadn't been in uniform. As it was, he just looked at her, and she looked at him, neither of them saying a word.

Suddenly, for no apparent reason, one of the boys picked up the tin soldier and tossed him into the stove. The goblin must have put him up to it.

The tin soldier stood in the flames. The heat was intense, but he wasn't really sure where it came from, the fire or his love. And though his brilliant uniform was worn and faded, whether this was due to his journey or his sorrow, no one could say.

He looked at the dancer. She looked back at him. Even as he began to melt, he remained steadfast, standing as straight as possible, with his rifle on his shoulder.

A door opened. A gust of wind caught the paper dancer and she flew like a sylph straight to the tin soldier's side.

She burst into a blaze and was gone.
He melted down into a little lump.

The next day, when the house-
maid emptied the ashes, she found
the tin soldier in the shape of a
heart. Of the lovely dancer all that
remained was her spangle, and that
was burned as black as coal.